Call Me Gorgeous!

Written by

Giles Milton

Illustrated by

Alexandra Milton

BOXER BOOKS

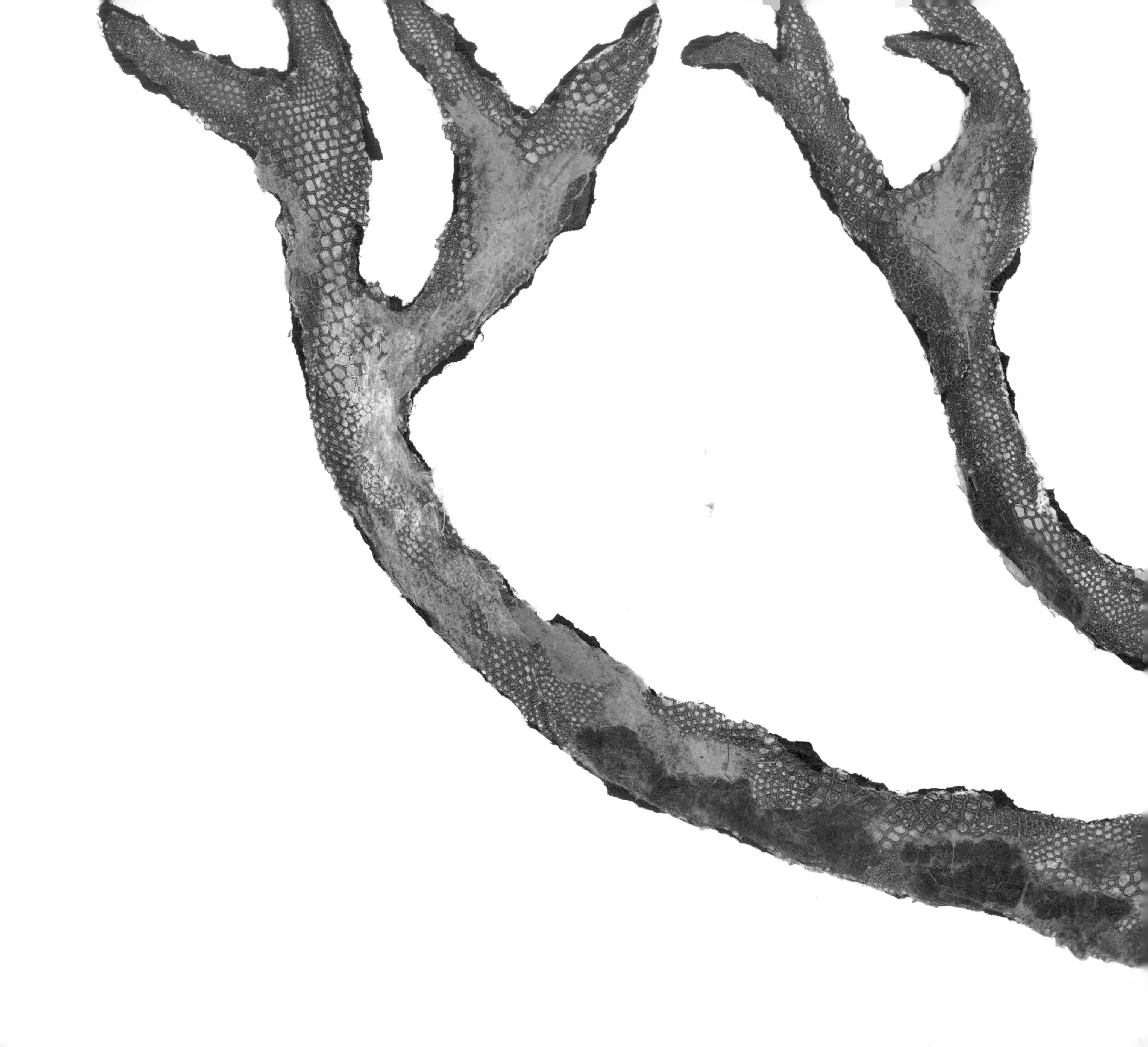

I've got
reindeer antlers

and the ears of a pig.

A porcupine's spines

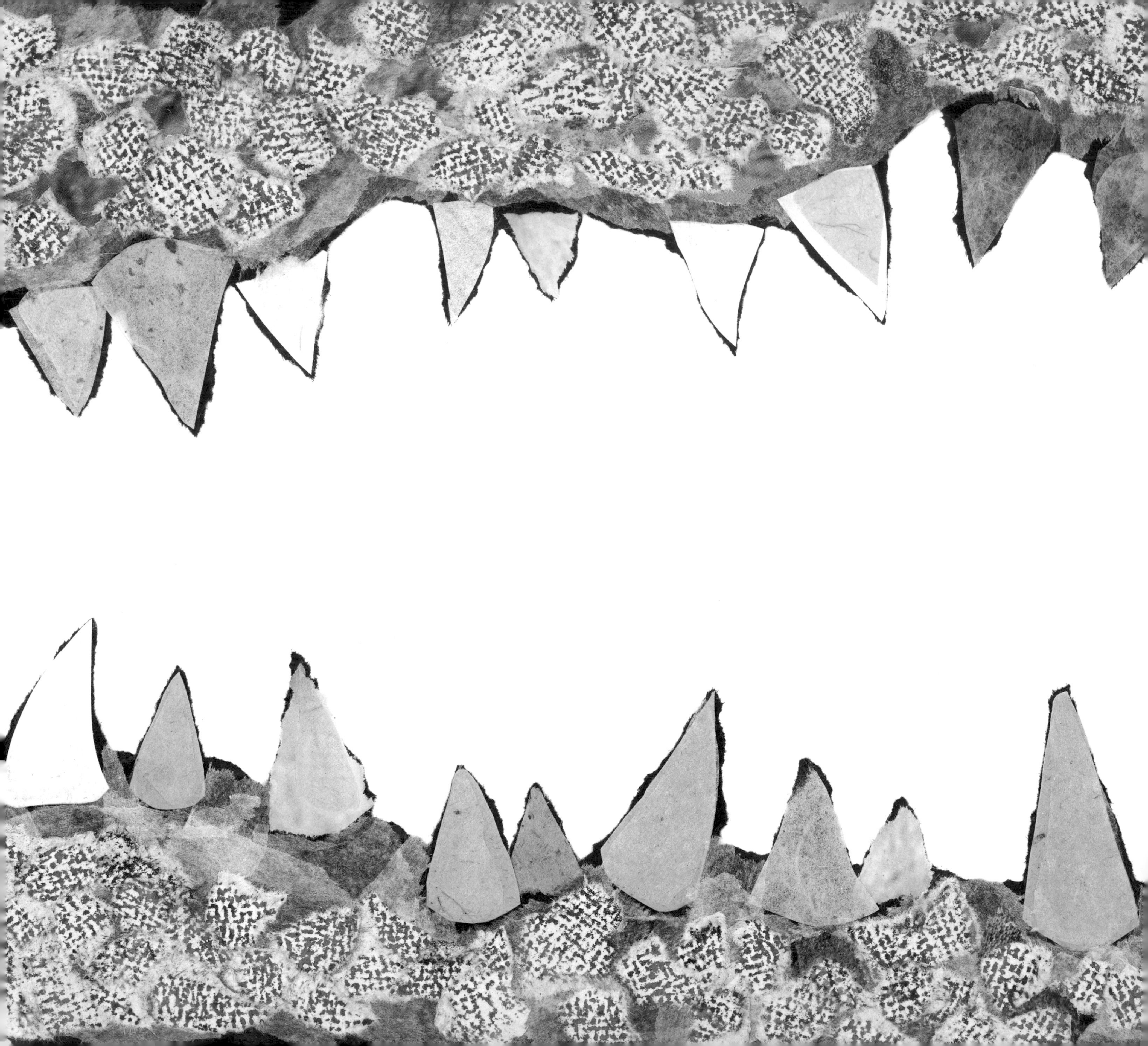

and a
crocodile's teeth.

A toucan’s beak

a flamingo's neck

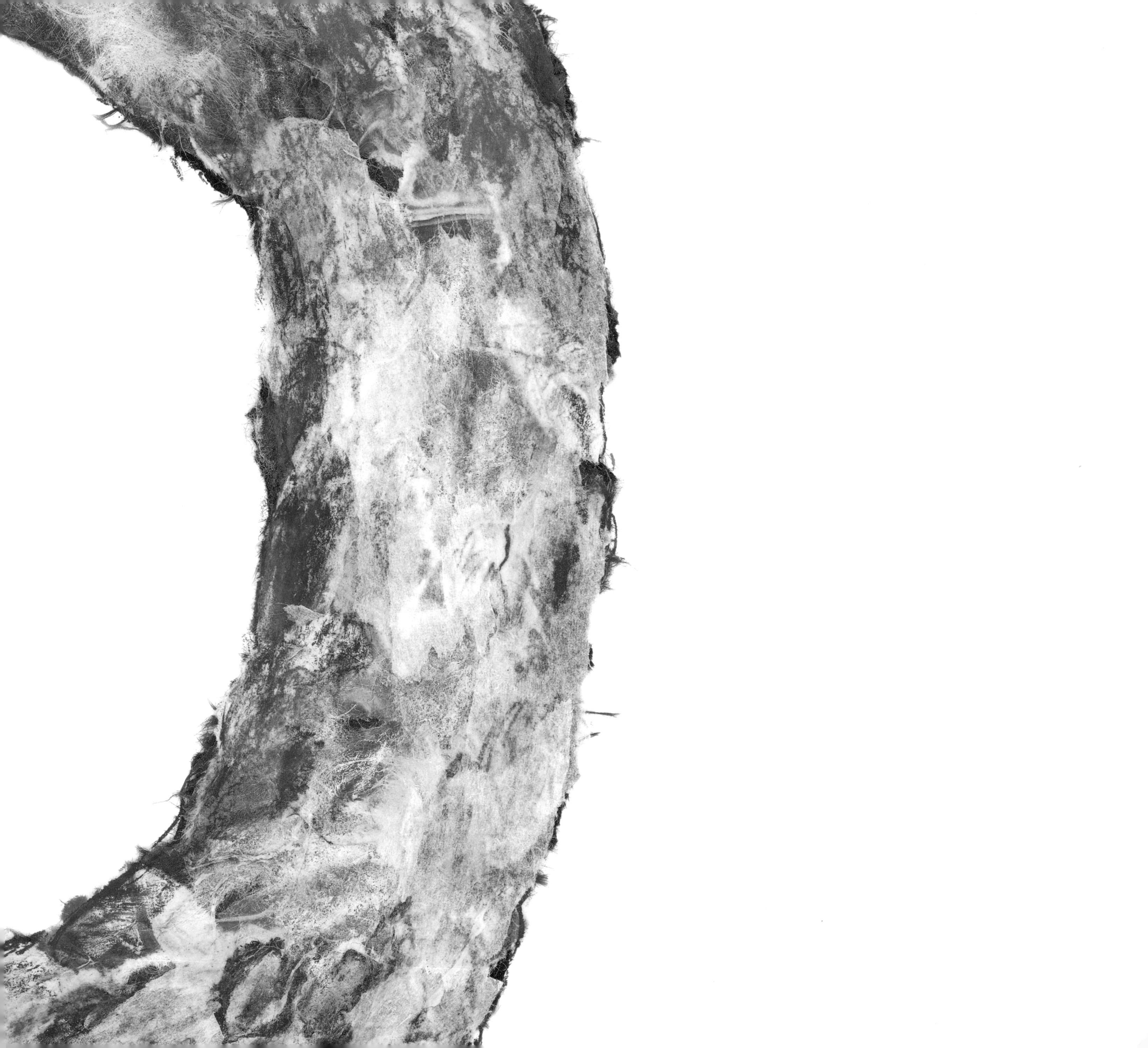

and a
rooster's feet.

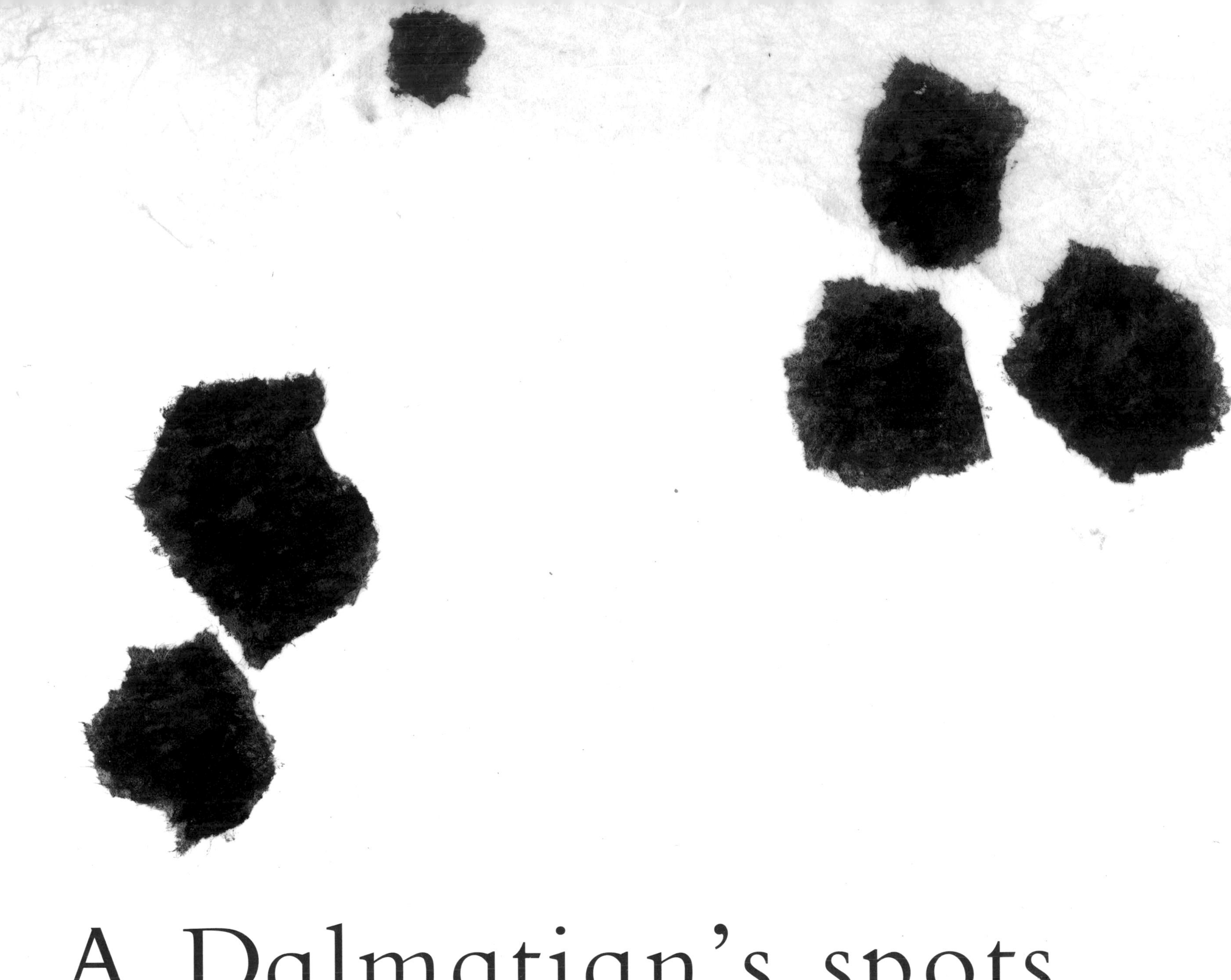

A Dalmatian's spots

and a
chameleon's tail.

The wings of a bat

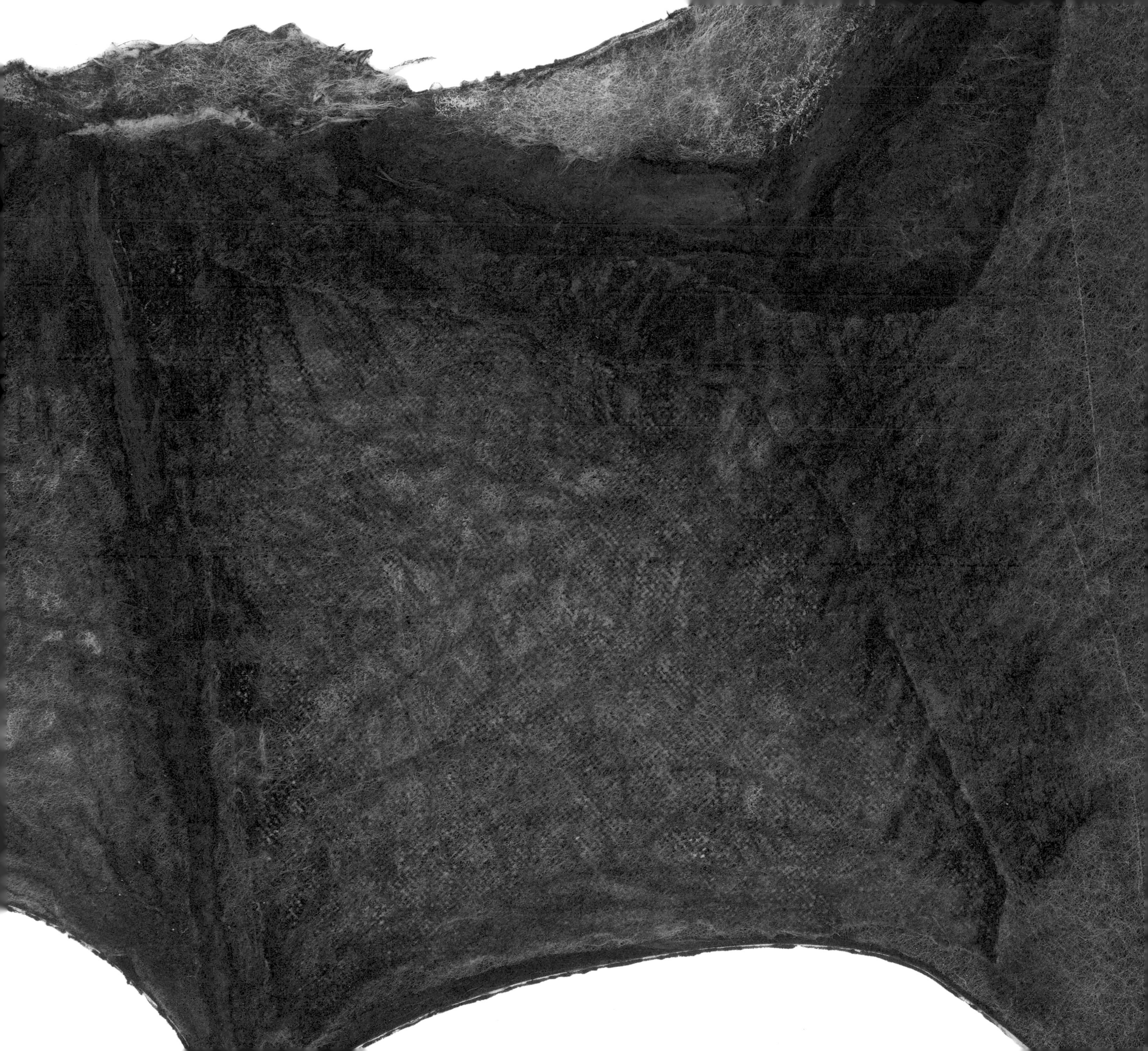

and the
eyes of a frog.

I’m a reinde-piggy-
porcu-croco-touca-
flami-roos-dalma-
chameleo-
bat-frog.

But . . .

you can call me

GORGEOUS!

For Madeleine, Héloïse, Aurélia—all gorgeous.
Giles and Alexandra Milton

First American edition published in 2009 by Boxer Books Limited.

Distributed in the United States and Canada by Sterling Publishing Co., Inc. 387 Park Avenue South, New York, NY 10016-8810

First published in Great Britain in 2009 by Boxer Books Limited.
www.boxerbooks.com

 Library of Congress Cataloging-in-Publication Data available.

The illustrations were created using color pencils and handmade paper from around the world. The text is set in Bembo Schoolbook.

ISBN 978-1-906250-71-3

1 3 5 7 9 10 8 6 4 2

Printed in China

All of our papers are sourced from managed forests and renewable resources.

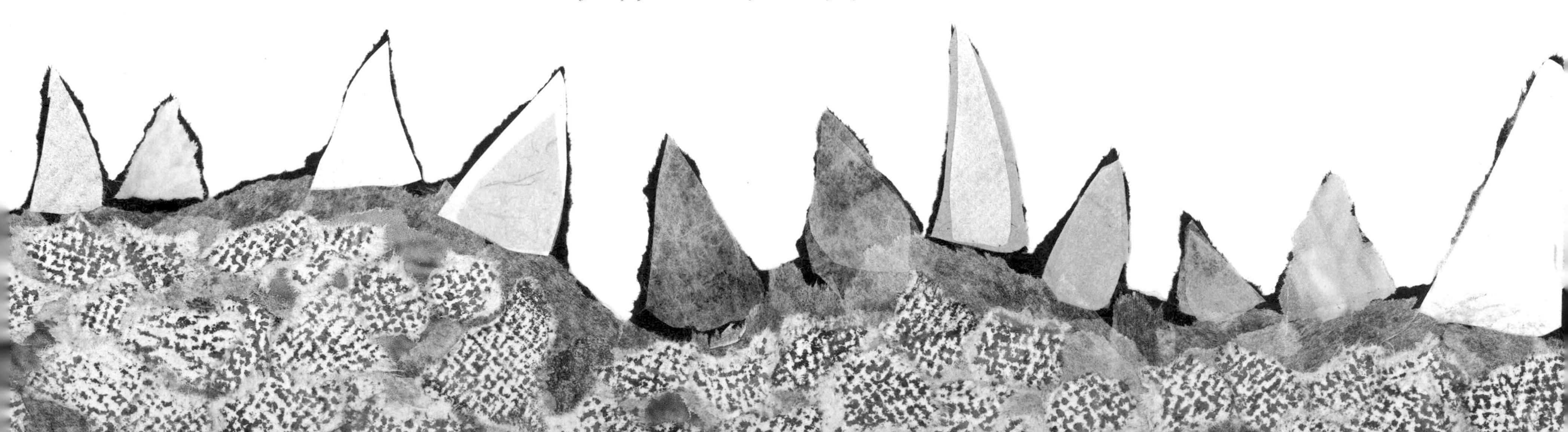